For Gemma, Hazel, Dave and Bethan

This edition produced for
The Book People Ltd,
Hall Wood Avenue, Haydock,
St Helen's, WA11 9UL

ISBN 1 85613 705 8

Printed in China

THE
BIGGEST BEAR

TED SMART

One evening, Toby was bouncing up and down on his bed. He looked at his shadow on the wall. It looked like a great big bear, jumping up and down next to him.

"I bet that's the biggest bear in the world!" he said, and he carried on bouncing till his daddy came to tuck him up in bed.

Next morning, Toby asked his daddy if the shadow bear was the biggest bear in the world.

"Oh, no," said Daddy. "There's a much bigger bear than that."

"Can we go and see him?" asked Toby.

"You'll have to wait until later," said Daddy. "First we have to go to the shops."

At the shops, Toby saw a great big
chocolate bear in a sweet shop window.
  "Is that the biggest bear in the world?"
he asked.
  "Oh, no," said Daddy. "There's a much
bigger bear than that."

"When can we see him?" asked Toby.
"Later," said Daddy. "First you
have to go to playschool."

At playschool Toby painted a picture. He wanted to paint a really big bear, but the paper was too small.

"It's still a very nice bear," said Daddy, when he picked Toby up. "And you'll see the biggest bear in the world later on. Come on, now. Let's go to the park."

At the park, Toby saw a huge bear made of stone. It was a fountain, and water poured out from its mouth.

"Is that the biggest bear in the world?" Toby asked.

"Oh, no," said Daddy. "The biggest bear's much bigger than that."

"Will we see him soon?" asked Toby.

"Quite soon," said Daddy. "Let's go and get an ice cream."

On the other side of the park they found a funfair.

"There he is!" shouted Toby. "That must be the biggest bear!"

"Oh, no," laughed Daddy. "He's big, but the biggest bear in the world is much bigger."

Toby shook paws with the big bear, and they walked on.

On the way home, Toby and his daddy stopped to look at an enormous balloon bear, floating above the town.
"There can't be a bigger bear than that!" said Toby, but Daddy just grinned.

Back at home, Daddy gave Toby his dinner.
"Is there really a bigger bear than
the balloon bear?" asked Toby.
"Yes," said Daddy. "A much, much
bigger one."
"But where does he live, if he's so big?"
asked Toby.
"I'll give you a clue," said Daddy.
"He lives above our heads. Can you
guess where?"
"Is he in the attic?" asked Toby.
"Is he on the roof?"
But Daddy just shook his head.

At last it was bedtime, and Toby still hadn't guessed where the biggest bear lived.

"I don't believe there is a biggest bear," he said sadly, and he trudged upstairs to bed.

A moment later, Daddy came into Toby's room.

"Don't be sad, Toby," he said. "You couldn't see the biggest bear during the day, because he only comes out at night. Would you like to see him now? He's just outside."

"Is he scary?" asked Toby.

"No," said Daddy. "He's not scary at all."

Daddy led Toby down the stairs and out into the garden.

"Look up at the sky!" he said. "Do you see those bright stars?" Toby gazed up into the darkness. "That group of stars is called the Great Bear," Daddy said. "Can you see his tail? And his paws?"

"Oh!" said Toby. "He was right above our heads all the time! That really is the biggest bear in the whole world!"